W9-DCY-093

Jamie Lee Curtis
&
Laura Cornell

JOANNA COTLER BOOKS
An Imprint of HarperCollins*Publishers*

Big Words

for Little People

Our BIG WORD is GRATITUDE to the TALENTED and SUPPORTIVE Heidi Schaeffer, Phyllis Wender and Kelly Curtis, and the INCOMPARABLE HarperCollins team: Karen Nagel, Alyson Day, Carla Weise, Kathryn Silsand, Lucille Schneider and Dorothy Pietrewicz.

—J.L.C. & L.C.

Big Words for Little People

Printed in the U.S.A.

For information address HarperCollins Children's Books, a division of HarperCollins Publishers, 1350 Avenue of the Americas, New York, NY 10019.
www.harpercollinschildrens.com

Library of Congress Cataloging-in-Publication Data is available.
ISBN 978-0-06-112759-5 (trade bdg.) — ISBN 978-0-06-112760-1 (lib. bdg.)

Designed by Carla Weise
1 2 3 4 5 6 7 8 9 10
❖
First Edition

For Joanna
—J.L.C. & L.C

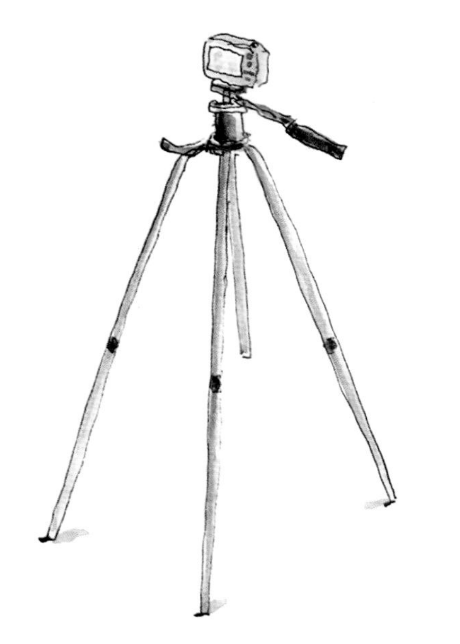

"Gray Mood"
WORLD'S LARGEST PUZZLE series
Spring in the Air
JULY
The RED of RED, WHITE & BLUE
February "Too Cold Outside"
Shoe of the Month Club
Curtain Dress KIT
Authentically Alpine series
Additional apron fabric
As seen in
Cut 'n' Tape
Authentically Alpine series
Favorite Things

I know some Big Words.
I'll teach them to you.
Although you are small,
you can use Big Words too.

BIG WORDS
aren't scary.
They're big fun to learn.
I was taught once
and now it's your turn.

If you need some time
to just be alone,
for doing weird dancing,
to sit still as a stone,
if someone is there
and you need to pee,
then say loud
and clear,

"Hey, I need
PRIVACY!"
ANTI PLAGUE with aloe
Masque of Beauty
GLOWY TEETH WITH BLEACH AND ANTIBIOTICS
32 oz
LARGE FAMILY SIZE

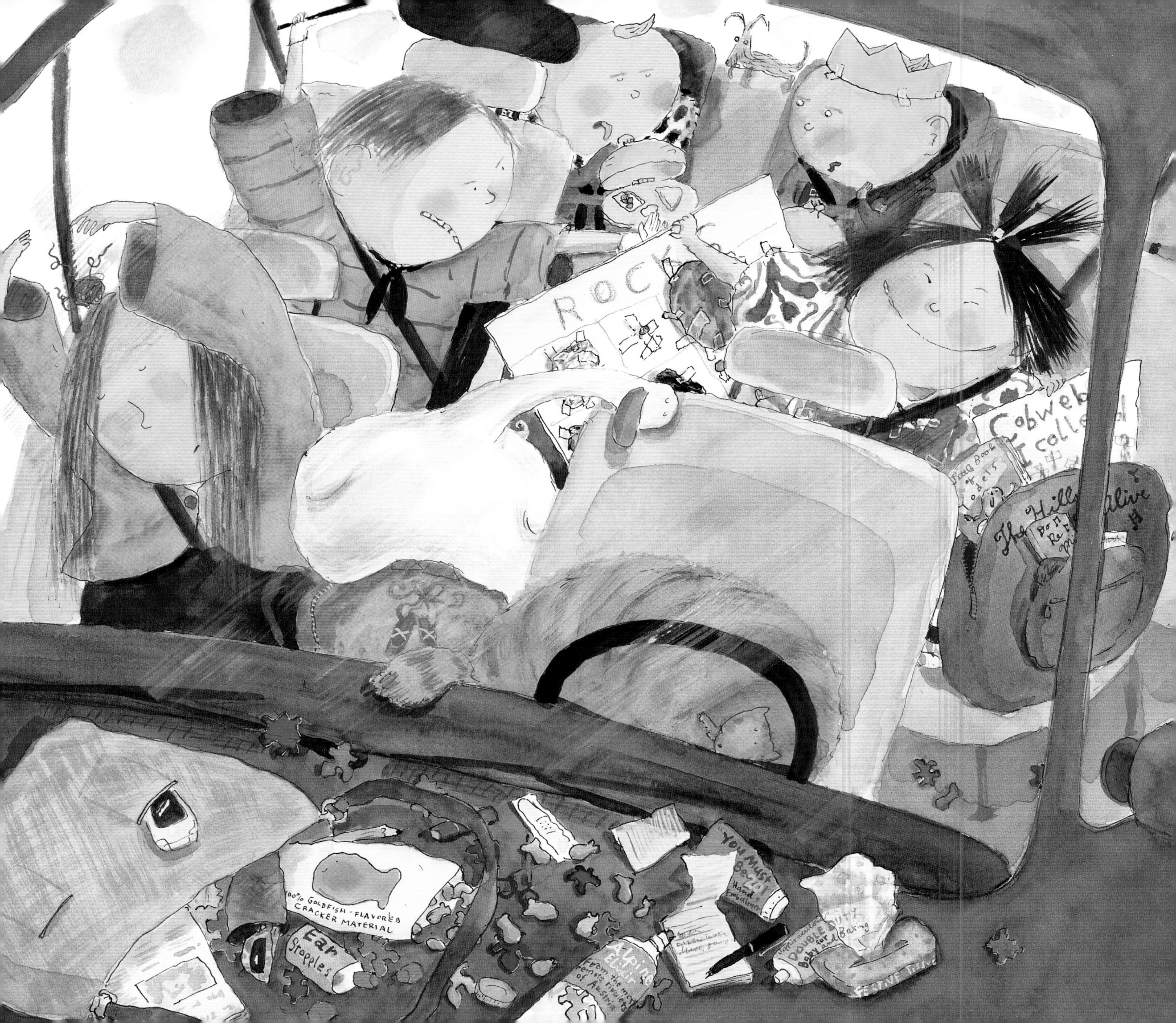
ROCK
100% GOLDFISH-FLAVORED CRACKER MATERIAL
Ear Stopples
Alpine Elixir
From the most remote rivulets of Austria
You Must Be
Hand Embalmer
DOUBLE DUTY for Baby and Baking
FESTIVE Tissue

When Mommy can't fasten the brand-new car seat,
and the twins don't like what they got to eat—
"This is

Mom says to us. "*Please!*
We can't leave for school
till you help find the keys."

If you answer right when you spell a Big Word,
your teacher might shout,

"STUPENDOUS! SUPERB!"

And then you can **CELEBRATE**—laugh and have fun—
'cause you've worked really hard to get the job done.

When you are at school
and you get into trouble
for chewing your gum,
then exploding a bubble,
and you stay inside
when your friends get to play,
your
CONSEQUENCE is
no recess that day.

HAVE YOU FED JUDY TODAY?
MON
TUES
WED
THURS
JUDY'S
Come home
MISSING

When Dad takes us shopping
to buy new shoes,
and all of us shout,
"This one I choose!"

and the salesman looks angry—
he's pretty
IRATE—

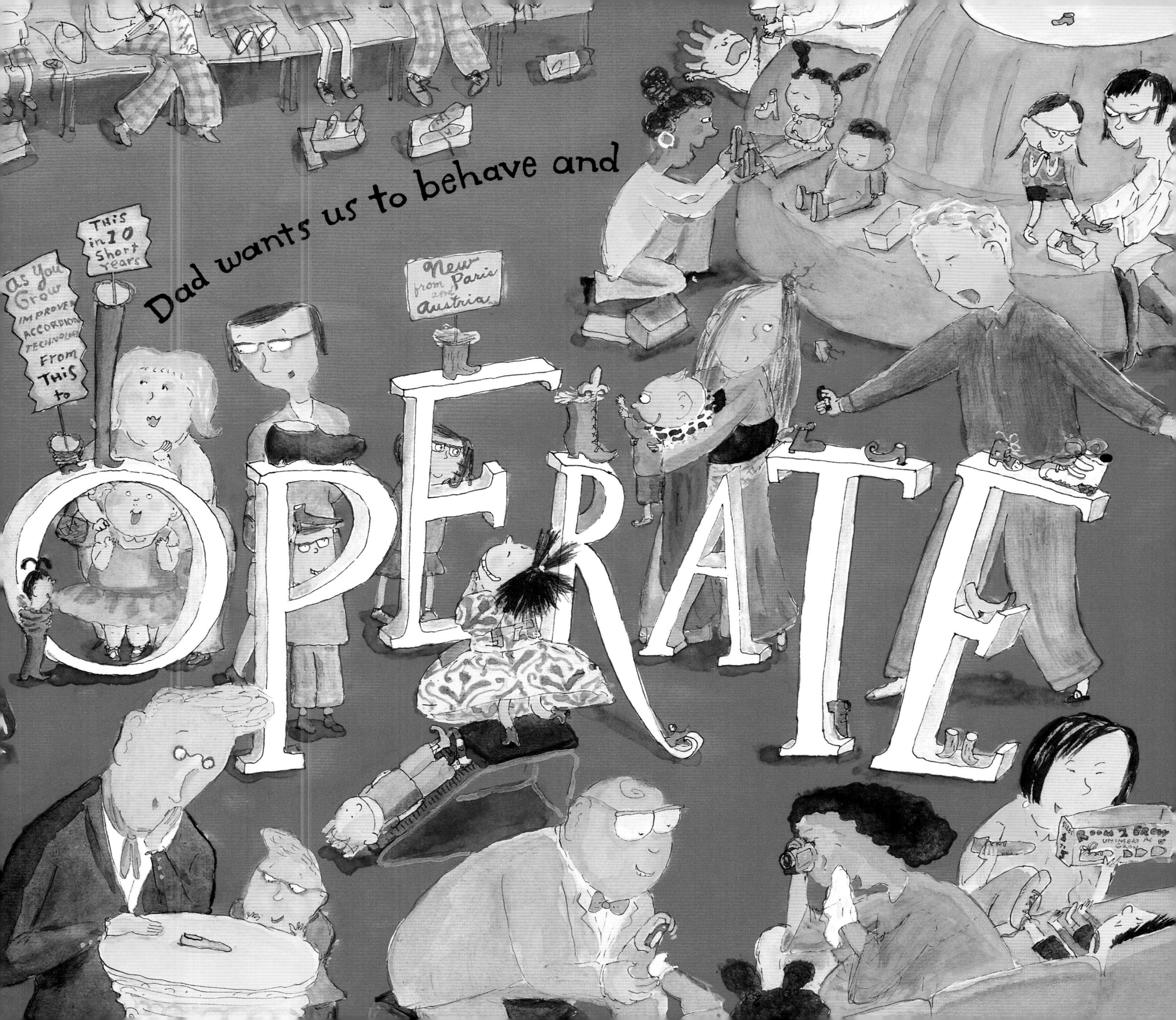

Dad wants us to behave and

OPERATE

When something is perfectly right for your age,
like TV and music, toys all the rage,
when a G-rated movie's the one that you seek,
APPROPRIATE is the word Mom will speak.

But many things are too old for you
that lots of your friends may still get to do.
INAPPROPRIATE is the word our mom picks
if you want to watch PG-13 when you're six.

When you wait and you wait for your chance at a turn
and your feet are both hot and are starting to burn
and there's still
a long way to the
front of the line,

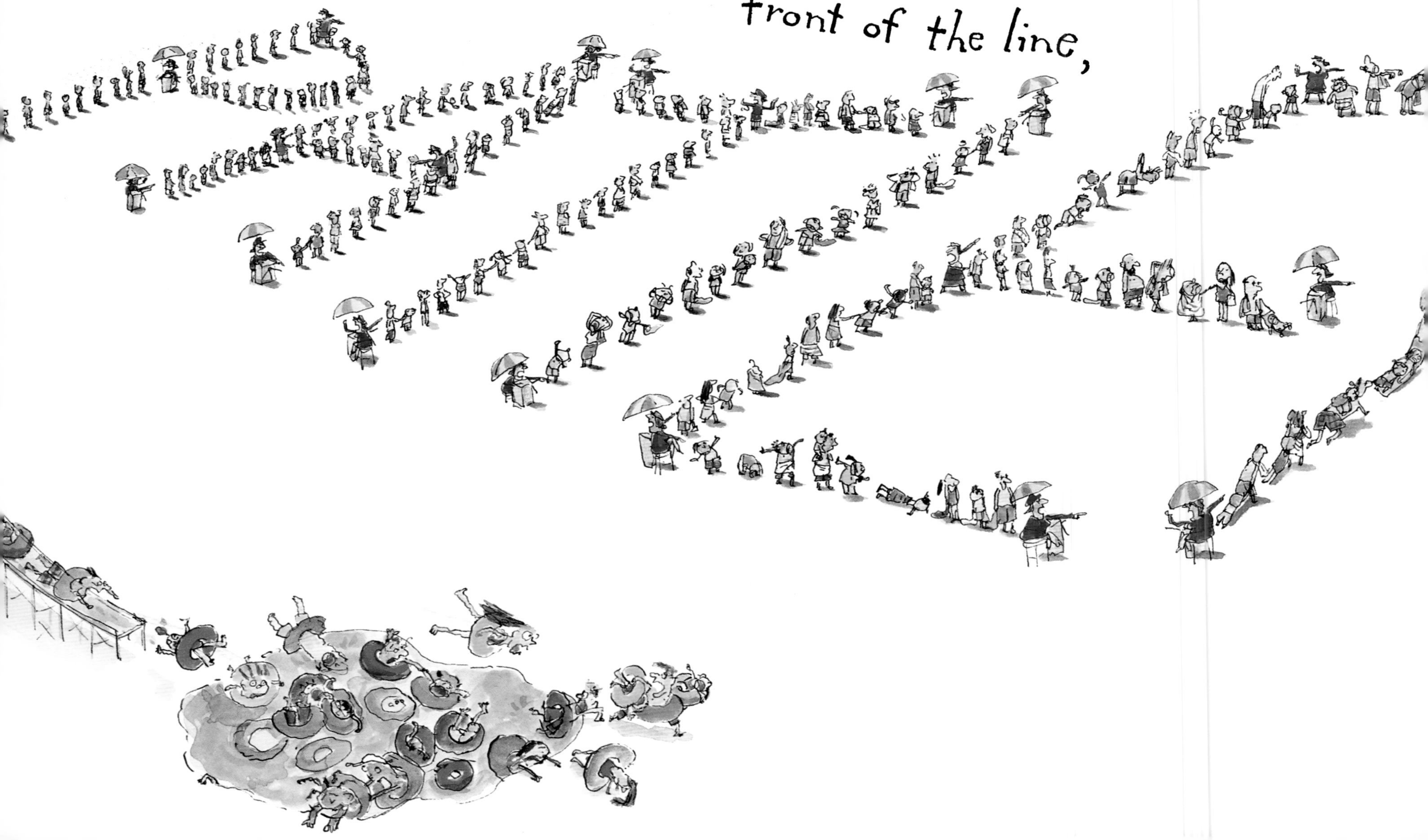

PATIENCE is the word you must try to find.

3-WEEK CRUST
DELICATE POTS + PANS
MEND AND POLISH
Rx SANDBLAST
START
AMAZING STICK-TO-ITSELF TECHNOLOGY
THE BREAKFAST OF COSMONAUTS
Space Cereal
Young Set BEVERAGE
Healthy Kitchen

mixing stuff up from the kitchen to drink
that looks really gross and has a big stink,
as our green-snotted brother's nose starts to get picked—

"DISGUSTING!"

you'd cry.
(It means **yucky**
and **ick**!)

To **UNDERSTAND** means you know when we say,
"A street is for cars! It's not safe to play!"

You understand
cows make milk and not juice,
that you don't run on "Duck"
but you do run on "Goose."

INCONSIDERATE
is the word Dad would pick
if you woke up Mom
when she's feeling sick.

But if you brought her
a flower and tea,
a **CONSIDERATE** person
is what he would see.

"I'm **RESPONSIBLE**," you say
when you pick up your toys

and walk our dog, Leo,
and try not to make noise.

Responsible people try not to forget
to water Mom's bonsai or the table to set.

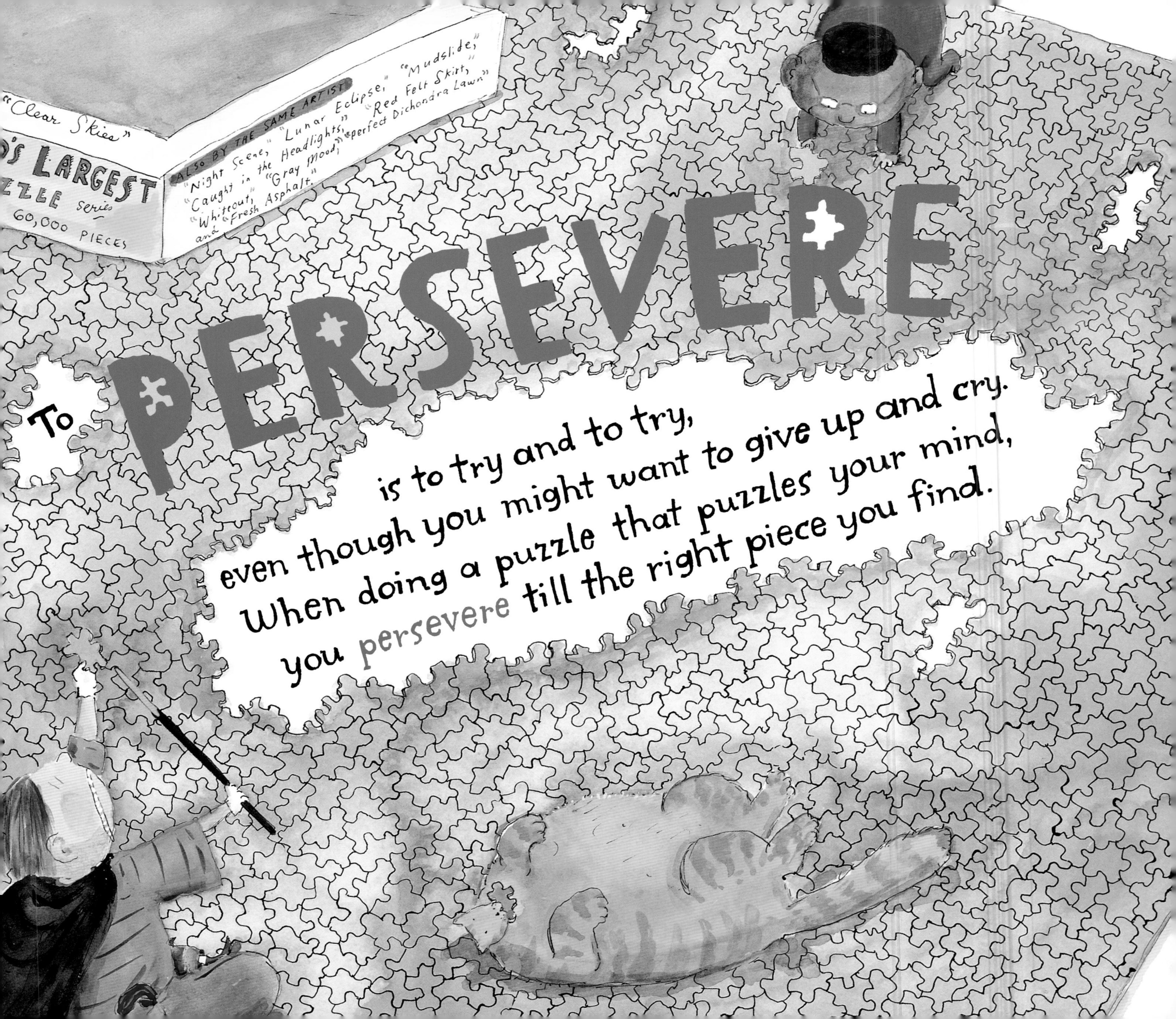

To **PERSEVERE**

is to try and to try,
even though you might want to give up and cry.
When doing a puzzle that puzzles your mind,
you persevere till the right piece you find.

DIFFERENT means nobody's ever the same.

All bodies are different and so are all brains.

Different is what makes this world so great.

Different is never something to hate.

But not all Big Words
are as **long** as the rest.
There are three—
though short—
that I love the best.

FAMILY is where we all belong,
keeping us safe, making us strong.
Family is yours, no matter—whatever!—
we care about you forever and ever.

RESPECT is the way we all treat each other—
mother to father, father to mother;
brother to sister,
sister to brother,
and brother
and sister
and sister
and brother . . .

Kat
BEFORE

Love

is the biggest **BIG** word of all.
Four little letters that help you walk tall.
Love is your family, your siblings, your friends.
Love is your ocean without any end.

See, Big Words are easy. How well you've done!
Now go off and have some really great fun.
And next time a grown-up thinks you don't have sense,
show them with Big Words your

INTELL

IGENCE!

my
favorite
things